*02

RENO

!111**211**-000++=0==+++==+=+=++*+===-++=+=

ALERT.ALert.ALER
-T.ALERT The
ENERGY ROUTER is
in critical
ERROR.ERROR
W-WHAT THA...?
send in
some
GUARD'S
NOOOW!!!!
WHER'E
UNDER ATTACK
BAM
BOOM
MOMMY-
HELP MEE!!
O-OH NO THE
SHIP IS
CRASHING
IDIOT
you're Grown
FOUND
it
Where is
It.?
HEh... IT seem's like
Those no Brainer's is
still srtuggling to
protect their precious
low formed ship
yahahah how
reasurring.

CHAPT·25
INTERNAL
STRUGGLE

A FOE WHO WILL SOON HAVE HER NAME KNOWN ON PLANET EARTH IN ABOUT 18,00 MILES AND 2,657 YEARS,ALTHOUG IN EARTH IT'S ABOUT 42YRS just WHO IS THIS MYSTERIOUS WOMAN··? AND WHAT IS HER INTENTIONS·

NOW BACK TO WHERE WE LEFT OFF SINCE RENO DEFEATED THE PETTY THIEF ZUKO ALTHOUGH SOMTHING UNUSUAL IS ABOUT TO HAPPEN.

TSS
TSS
TSS
GYAAA-AAAAAAAAAAAAAA
GRRAA It's like I was STRUCK by lightning.
HUFF HUFF
AKC
I have no energy, I feel like my body and mind is shutting down, im barley huff huff holding on to a GRASP

MEOW you SEEM TIRED, LOOK'S LIKE I NEED TO PUT YOU OUT OF YOU'R MISERY.

LEG PIER-CE.
GAH.

HUFF
HUFF

WHAM

SWING
SLICE
GAAAAA
-AAAA.

AS LONG AS I AM STILL STANDING, YOU CAN NEVER TEAR OR CUT ME DOWN.
YOU HEAR ME.

LET'S PUT THAT TO THE TEST.
!
WHAA AAAAA WHAA..
PLEASE SIR,HE-LP ME
IM SCARE-D

HEEEEEEEE-
LP ME PLEASE
MOMMY,DAD-
DY IM SORRY
I TREATED YOU
horri
ble.

TSSP

HMP.

w-what

TSSP
SNIFF

MEOW he fell for it.

ZOOM

GUH...
DAMN

LOOK
OUT
SIR!!!!!!!

It
was a
trap
all
along.

FHSN

SMAASH
yank
swoosh
Grg
Blaaak
crack
gaaaaa
she
smashe
-d her
heels,
into
my arm

CAT
SCRA
-TCH

I have to save him no matter what.

you can't just make things up as you please.

SCRATCH
scratch

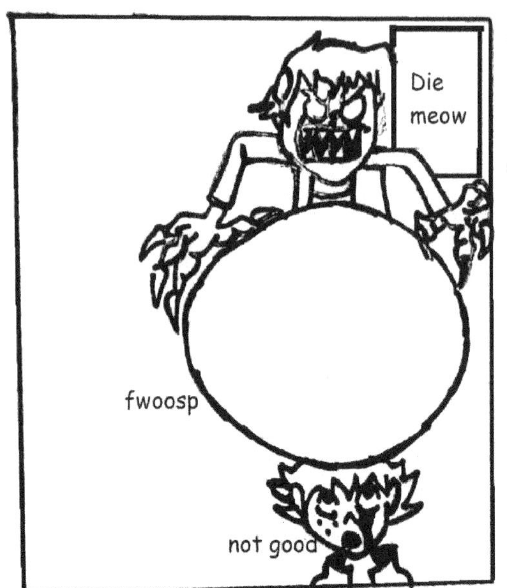
Die
meow
fwoosp
not good

A bomb
h-how
can she.?
huff
huff

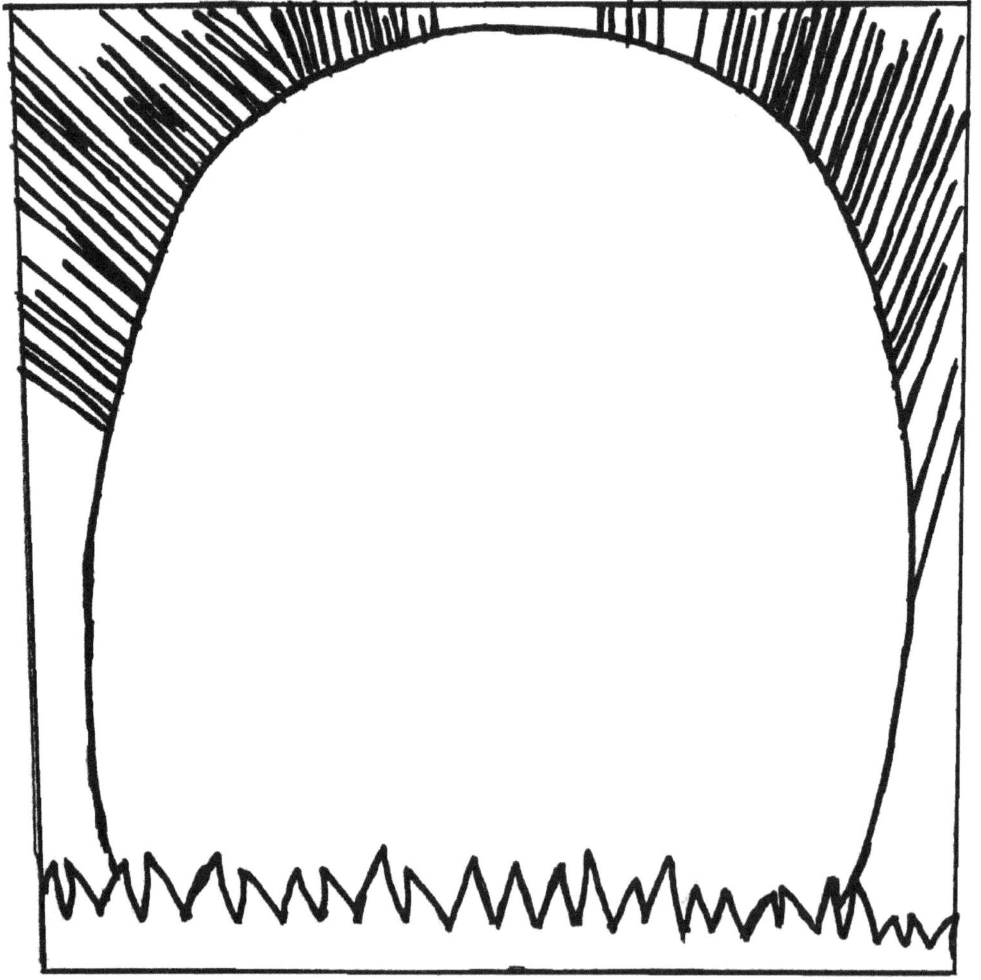

BOOOOOMMM

SABRINA, LAUNCHES A EXSPLOSIVE BOMB THAT HAS RENO CAUGHT UP IN IT, STRUGGLING TO FIND A WAY TO BEAT HER AND SAVE THE HELPLESS BOY WHO SABRINA KID NAPPED, TIME IS TICKING FOR THE FATE OF THE CITIZEN'S AND THE WHOLE ENTIRE WORLD.

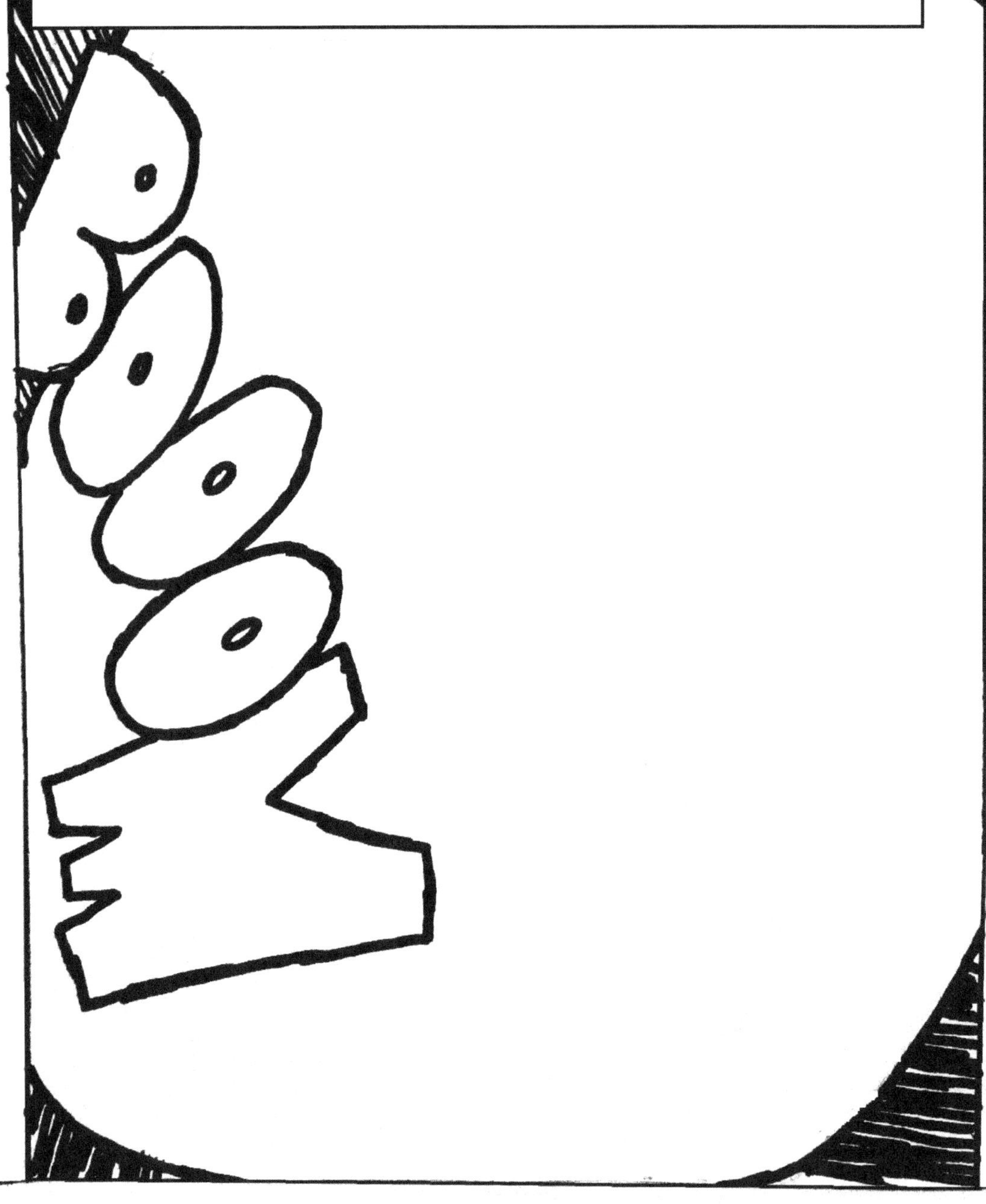

GAH

BOOM

YOU'RE MY SAVIOR MY HOPE..

DON'T DIE SIR.

DAMN, THIS BRAT IS ANNOYING HE DOESN'T SHUT UP GUESS I HAVE TO KILL HIM.

BLAAK
BALL
EXSPLOSI
-ON OF
DEATH

AHHH
HHHH.
MEANWHILE...
virtual
Man THE
DIGITAL
HERO
AGE:FINITY
...

huh, just who might you be.
I'M AN OLD FRIEND of yours i want to HELP.
VM

shut up i don't got any friends
swoosh

VM

S-SHE'S SO STRONG I DON'T THINK I HAVE ANY ENERGY LEFT AFTER I DEFEATED THE THIEF MY
WHOLE BODY JUST FROZE, I WAS GETTING SHOCK ALL
over my body heh that's one powerfule form.
Listen I am virtural man from another world, well another video game world that is i was flying and heard you screaming.

I SEE A CAVE
UP AHEAD
WHITE
HAIRE BOY.!!
HEY YOU
JERK THE
NAME'S
RENO NOT
WHITE
HAIR BOY.

YOU DAMN BASTARD, I
SAID STOP CALLING ME
WHITE HAIRE BOY.
THIS IS WHAT
HAPPENED...
TO SABRINA WHITE
HAIR BOY, BUT FIRST I
HAVE TO TALK ABOUT
HER PAST.
VM

SABRINA MARIBEL AGE:8

A.K.A LIL BEL

meow-
meow-
meow.

YOU'RE MY BEST FURIEND.
HEY LITTLE KITTY ARE YOU LOST.? OOH YOUR SO SO CUTE I WANNA TAKE YOU HOME, NO I AM GONNA TAKE YOU HOME.
MEOW

LIFE IS SWEETER A PRECIOUS GEM IS WHAT YOU ARE YOU'RE MOMMY'S BRIGHT AND SHINING STAR

welcome home
YOU'RE GONNA LOVE YOUR NEW HOME, MOMMY IS VERY NICE
MARIBEL HOUSEHOLD
YEAR: 1980

meow
mom
Im home.
WHAA

BECAUSE I
LOVE YOU.

HEY BRAT, JUST WHAT THE HELL ARE YOU DOING BRINGING A CAT IN HERE
ALTHOUGH YOU ARE A MISTAKE REGRET IT.

MOM BECAUS -S YOU'RE SPEACI LE TO ME,YOU 'RE MY PARTNE R
MY SUN.

Bomb Collar
sniff
sniff
MOM WHY WHY WHY.
BEEB
BEEB
click
click
BEEB
BEEB

I WILL TEAR EVERY SINGLE SPIRIT OUT OF YOU, YOU'RE JUST A WORTHLESS LITTLE BRAT WHO'S BORN TO BE NOTHING It's REALLY FUNNY ON HOW YOU THINK YOU'RE CUTE WHEN REALLY YOU'RE NOT, HA-HA-HA-HA-HA-HA SAY LET'S SEE HOW MANY BEAT'S YOU CAN SURVIVE ALTHOUGH, IT WOULDN'T MAKE A DIFFERENCE ANYWAY'S BECAUSE YOUR WEAK AND PATHETIC,TO HAVE A DAUGHTER LIKE YOU MAKES ME WANNA END MY OWN LIFE.
FACE IT SCUM THIS IS YOUR FUTURE, YOU'RE PURPOSE, YOU'RE DESTINY THERE'S NO OTHER PATH FOR YOU TO TAKE ONLY DESPAIRE NOT EVEN THE MAN HIMSELF.

Sabrina, is crying for the mom's approval of her, it's been about an hour passed and sabrina still has the bomb collar around her neck shocking her to death.
MOM
0

AAAAAAAAAAAAAAAAAAAAAA
AAAAAAAAAAAAAAAAAAAAAA
AAAAAAAAAAAAAAAAAAAAAA
AAAAAAAAAAAAAAAAAAAAAA
AAAAAAAAAAAAAAAAAAAAAA
AAAAAAAAAAAAAAAAAAAAA
Drip
DRip
Drip
Drip

BOOM
say you ain't so pretty no more haha.

BLOOD-BLOOD-
BLOOD I LOVE IT
HAhA BLEED
somemore.
IN FACT
GET
OUTT-A
MY
HOUSE!

SHUT UP JUST SHUT THE HELL UP ALREADY .

please I wanna stay with mom.

MOMM'Y LOVES ME, YES WHY WHY WHY HAHAHA YES GOOD GIRL,I AM A GOOD heh
HAHAHA HA HA HA HA HA HA HA HA HA
Drip
Drip
DRIP

JUST GIVE
ME YOU'R
HAND.

such futile talent you are very special, together we can show this whole entire world just how important you're.

RAAARAA
RAAAAA
AAAAAHH
AAAAAH

THAT'S HORRIBLE
I KNEW SHE
WASN'T A BAD
PERSON.

RAVEN SCAR

IM GROWING TIRED
OF
thes-
e
games

SHE NEED'S MY HELP, YOU MAY HAVE FAIELD TO SAVE HER DOESN'T MEAN I'LL SIT HERE AND GIVE UP LIKE YOU DID.
w-whaaat
meow I found ya'l
DON'T WORRY I'll BE FINE, I PRO....
WAIT RENO,LET ME HANDLE THIS.!!

hang on, RENO

STOP PLEASE,YOU DON'T HAVE TO BE LIKE YOUR MOM ANYMORE,SHE CAN'T HURT YOU NO LONGER YOU CAN LIVE FREELY IT'S NOT THE SAME AS WHEN YOU WERE A INOCCENT KID, YOU DON'T HAVE TO BE AFRAID OF THOSE HORRIBLE

TO BE CONTINUED...
poor boy are you hurting,are you suffering die being a worthless shrimp who have no reason to be in this world just
RAAAA
NGH

www.ingramcontent.com/pod-product-compliance
Lightning Source LLC
LaVergne TN
LVHW082300150826
845677LV00009B/1677